Published by Lothrop, Lee & Shepard Books
a division of William Morrow and Company, Inc.
1350 Avenue of the Americas, New York, NY 10019
www.williammorrow.com

First U.S. edition published in 1999.
PRINTED IN ITALY
2 4 6 8 10 9 7 5 3 1

Library of Congress Cataloging-in-Publication Data
McKee, David.
Elmer and the lost teddy/by David McKee.
p. cm.
Summary: Baby Elephant cannot get to sleep when he loses
his teddy bear, so Elmer sets out to find it.
ISBN 0-688-16912-0
[1. Elephants—Fiction. 2. Teddy bears—Fiction. 3. Toys—Fiction.
4. Lost and found possessions—Fiction.] I. Title.
PZ7.M19448Emn 1999 [E]—DC21 98-44729 CIP AC

ELMER AND THE LOST TEDDY

DAVID McKEE

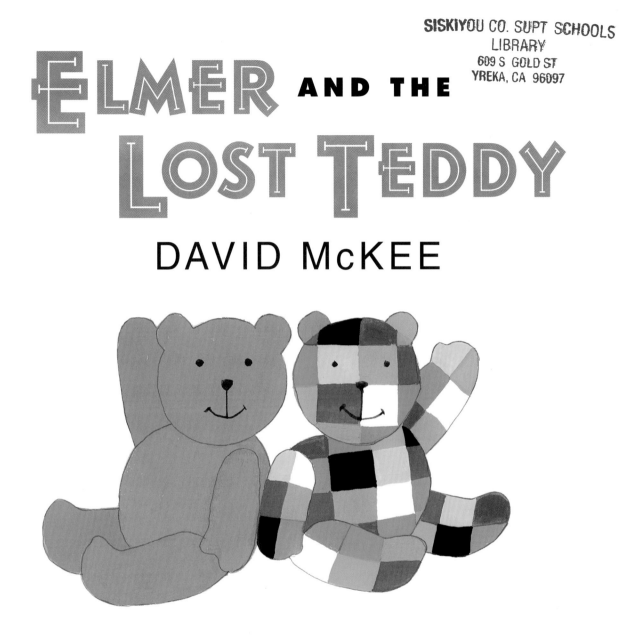

Lothrop, Lee & Shepard Books
NEW YORK

The sky was already dark and full of stars when Elmer,
the patchwork elephant, heard the sound of crying.
It was Baby Elephant.

"He can't sleep," said Mother Elephant. "He wants his
teddy. We took Teddy with us on a picnic, and somewhere
we lost it."

"Never mind," said Elmer. "He can borrrow my teddy tonight. Tomorrow I'll look for his."

Elmer hurried home for his teddy. As soon as Baby Elephant snuggled down with it, he fell fast asleep.

The next morning, Elmer set off in search of the lost teddy. He hadn't gone far when he met his cousin Wilbur. Wilbur was a ventriloquist. He could make his voice sound like it came from anywhere, and he loved to play tricks.

"Hello, Wilbur," said Elmer. "I'm looking for Baby Elephant's lost teddy. Have you seen it?"

"No," said Wilbur. His voice sounded like it came from Bird. "But if I find it, I'll call you."

A little later a voice said, "Hello, Elmer. Where are you going?" It was Lion.

"Baby Elephant has lost his teddy, and I'm looking for it," Elmer explained.

"Oh dear," said Lion. "Baby Lion would be very upset if he lost his teddy. If I find it, I'll call you. Maybe Tiger has seen it."

"Yoho! Tiger!" Elmer called as he came near Tiger's home.

"Ssssh, Elmer!" said Tiger. "The twins are asleep."

"Sorry," Elmer whispered. "Baby Elephant has lost his teddy. Have you seen it?"

"That's serious," said Tiger. "The twins wouldn't sleep without their teddies. If I find it, I'll call you."

All day long, Elmer went from animal to animal. All the young ones had *their* teddies, but none of them had seen Baby Elephant's teddy. They all said the same thing: "If we find it, we'll call you."

It was getting late, and Teddy was still lost.

I hope I find him soon, thought Elmer. It's nearly time for bed.

Just at that moment, he heard a shout. "Help! Help!" And then, "I'm lost! I'm lost!"

Elmer pushed through some bushes, and there, sitting under a tree, was a teddy bear.

"Please help me," said the teddy. "I want to go home. I can't sleep without my baby elephant."

"You can talk!" said Elmer in surprise. "But why isn't your mouth moving?"

Just then Wilbur appeared from the bushes.

Elmer laughed. "I've been tricked again," he said. "I should have known it was you making Teddy talk."

Wilbur chuckled. "I told you I'd call if I found Teddy,"
he said. "Come on. Let's take Teddy home. It's getting dark."

And the two cousins set off together, singing as they went.

Baby Elephant was excited to see his own teddy again.

Mother Elephant couldn't thank Elmer and Wilbur enough.

"Weren't you worried that Baby Elephant might want to keep *your* teddy?" Wilbur asked Elmer on their way home. "Your teddy is very different. It's special."

"But Wilbur, didn't you know?" said Elmer in surprise.
"You don't have to be *different* to be special. *All* teddies are
special—especially your own."